The Family Book

TOdd PARR

Megan Tingley Books
LITTLE, BROWN AND COMPANY
New York ·ɔ· An AOL Time Warner Company

ALSO BY TODD PARR:

The Best Friends Book

Big & Little

Black & White

The Daddy Book

Do's and Don'ts

The Feel Good Book

The Feelings Book

Funny Faces

Going Places

It's Okay to Be Different

The Mommy Book

My Really Cool Baby Book

The Okay Book

Otto Goes to Bed

Otto Goes to the Beach

Things That Make You Feel Good /
Things That Make You Feel Bad

This Is My Hair

Underwear Do's and Don'ts

Zoo Do's and Don'ts

First Edition

Library of Congress Cataloging-in-Publication Data

Parr, Todd.
  The family book / by Todd Parr. — 1st ed.
    p. cm.
  "Megan Tingley Books"
  Summary: Represents a variety of families, some big and some small,
some with only one parent and some with two moms or dads, some quiet
and some noisy, but all alike in some ways and special no matter what.
  ISBN 0-316-73896-4
  [1. Family—Fiction. 2. Individuality—Fiction.] I. Title
PZ7.P2447 Fam 2003
[E]—dc21   2002036843

10 9 8 7 6 5 4 3 2 1

TWP

Printed in Singapore

To my Family—who sometimes
did not understand me,
but encouraged me to
go after everything I wanted
even when we did not agree.
As I now realize—this takes
a lot of love to do.

—T.P.

Some families are big

Some families are small

Some families are the same color

Some families are different colors

All families like to HUG each other!

Some families live near each other

Some families live far from each other

Some families look alike

Some families look like their pets

All families are Sad when they lose someone they Love.

Some families have a
stepmom or stepdad and
stepsisters or stepbrothers

Some families adopt children

Some families have two
moms or two dads

Some families have one parent instead of two

All families like to celebrate special days together!

Some families eat the same things

Some families eat different things

Some families like to be quiet

Some families like to be clean

Some families like to be messy

Some families live in a
house by themselves

Some families share a house with other families

All families
each other

can help
be STRONG!

There are lots of different ways to be a family. Your family is special no matter what kind it is.

♡ Love, Todd